CORDUROY & COMPANY

a Don Freeman Treasury

With an introduction by Leonard S. Marcus

Viking

VIKING
Published by the Penguin Group
Penguin Putnam Books for Young Readers, 345 Hudson Street, New York, New York 10014, U.S.A.
Penguin Books Ltd, 27 Wrights Lane, London W8 5TZ, England
Penguin Books Australia Ltd, Ringwood, Victoria, Australia
Penguin Books Canada Ltd, 10 Alcorn Avenue, Toronto, Ontario, Canada M4V 3B2
Penguin Books (N.Z.) Ltd, 182-190 Wairau Road, Auckland 10, New Zealand
Penguin Books Ltd, Registered Offices: Harmondsworth, Middlesex, England

First published in 2001 by Viking, a division of Penguin Putnam Books for Young Readers.

3   5   7   9   10   8   6   4

LIBRARY OF CONGRESS CATALOGING-IN-PUBLICATION DATA
Freeman, Don.
Corduroy and company : a Don Freeman treasury / with an introduction by Leonard S. Marcus.
p. cm.
ISBN 978-0-670-03510-6 (Hardcover)
1. Children's stories, American. [1. Short stories.] I. Marcus, Leonard S., 1950- II. Title.
PZ7.F8747 Cp 2001
[E]—dc21
2001001030

Printed in China
Set in Minister Light

Book design by Edward Miller

Contents

Introduction

For Don Freeman (1908-1978) as for many American artists of the postwar baby-boom years, personal and professional life happily converged in the discovery of the picture book as an art form worth exploring. In 1948, Freeman, a respected Broadway theater-page illustrator and printmaker, left New York with his wife Lydia, a painter, to resettle in their native California. The following year, their only son, Roy, was born in Santa Barbara. Soon afterward, the couple coauthored the story that was to become their first picture-book collaboration, *Chuggy and the Blue Caboose* (1951). Although the Freemans originally intended *Chuggy* for home consumption, a librarian who read the manuscript encouraged them to publish it. Urged by their librarian friend to "start at the top," they submitted their story to May Massee of New York's Viking Press.

As the first junior-books editor both at Doubleday and at Viking, May Massee did indeed represent the peak of her profession. Since the 1920s, Massee had taken the lead in championing the ideal of the "book beautiful"—the picture book as an aesthetically refined and vibrant narrative art form designed especially for children. From her elegant Viking aerie with its carved wood ceiling bearing the motto "All things in moderation—including moderation," she guided the progress of such luminaries as Maud and Miska Petersham, Robert Lawson, Marjorie Flack, Kurt Wiese, Ludwig Bemelmans, Ingri and Edgar Parin d'Aulaire, William Pène du Bois, Marie Hall Ets, and Robert McCloskey. It was a badge of honor to be published by Massee; bearers of the badge routinely also won Caldecott Medals.

Massee would surely have recog-

nized Chuggy's coauthor as the *New York Times*'s and *Herald Tribune*'s long-time drama-page artist. She may also have known the Freemans' *Newsstand*, a self-published quarterly magazine of the 1930s and '40s featuring Don's spirited lithographs and occasional writings on the street theater of New York City life. Whatever her knowledge of their prior accomplishments, in taking on *Chuggy*, Massee clearly saw in that journeyman effort the promise of greater things to come. In a letter to Don Freeman written a year after publication, she urged the artist not to "spread [himself] too thin" by taking on illustration assignments from the Hollywood studios, and to "concentrate" on his next picture book. "I know this sounds like a lecture," Massee sternly declared, "and that's just what it is, because I want to see you do some of our best books."

Although friends back East puzzled over Freeman's apparent break with his Broadway past, Freeman himself considered picture-book making as a continuation of those earlier activities. As he told an interviewer: "There has to be an element of suspense to make you turn the page. That's really theater." While no longer absorbed in chronicling the performances of others, Freeman had found in the picture book a stage of his own, a charmed and intimate story-hour theater where the author and artist had near-total creative freedom and the best seats in the house belonged to children.

May Massee's faith was rewarded with a second Freeman collaboration that marked an inspired advance in narrative polish and sophistication. The first story to draw directly on Don Freeman's knowledge of the theater, *Pet of the Met* (1953) was a bravura performance that contemporary critics hailed as "distinguished." In *Pet*, the spotlight largely fell—as it had in the work of the artist's self-described "backstage-struck" New York years—on the side dramas at the periphery of the show the audience has come to see. In this and subsequent picture books, Freeman forged strong and sympathetic lines of identification between the lot of the performance world's unsung on- and offstage minor players and that of life's ultimate minor players—children.

Freeman's thoughtful, gentle, unpretentious picture books (solo efforts from then onward, as Lydia focused increasingly on her painting) mix dreamlike make-believe with comforting reminders of the rewards of friendship, the dignity of honest labor, and other home truths.

In *Pet of the Met*, it is casually assumed that a mouse can hold down a job as an opera prompter's page-turner. Not only that, Maestro Petrini is a refined mouse in tails who takes justifiable pride in the work by which he "earn[s] his daily cheese." In *Norman the Doorman* (1959), another cultured mouse, this one living in an art museum basement, not only leads his fellow creatures on tours of the premises but feels moved to create "something pleasing or beautiful" of his own. The windup toy *Beady Bear* (1954) swings into action, naturally enough, when a child turns the key, but then Beady does the unexpected: he opens a book and reads a passage about bears that sets him off on a journey of self-discovery. When, in

Corduroy (1968), another toy bear climbs down from his department-store shelf after closing time to take a walk, no explanation is offered, or needed, to account for his lifelike behavior. Children, Freeman knew, make similar leaps of imagination all the time.

Other Freeman stories poke good-natured fun at human shortcomings or highlight the small but absorbing dramas that take up most of our days. In *Dandelion* (1964), a cautionary tale, a dandyish fashion makeover renders a salt-of-the-earth lion unrecognizable to his friends. The lesson is clear: getting fancy with those you love is a recipe for loneliness. In *Mop Top* (1955), both sides of a familiar childhood battle of wits receive a sympathetic airing: the mother who thinks her son needs a haircut; the scruffy lad who, with Tom Sawyer-like insouciance, finds plenty to distract him en route to the dreaded chair.

The dachshund messenger of *Flash the Dash* (1973) delivers most of the telegrams entrusted to him on time, but when spring arrives he cannot help giving in to the urge to

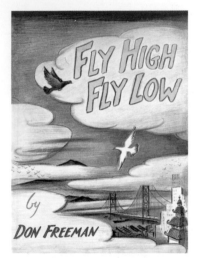

stretch out in the sun for a nice long nap. Who—Freeman suggests with forgiving wink and a nod—can blame him?

Other matters cannot wait. When Sid and Midge, the pigeon protagonists of *Fly High Fly Low* (1957), unexpectedly get separated from each other, Sid searches all San Francisco until he and his mate are reunited. This poignant tale of loyalty and love, for which Freeman received a 1958 Caldecott Honor, doubles as the artist's homage to the City by the Bay and brims with details of street and harbor life, lovingly observed.

Freeman had a lifelong soft spot for corny puns and gags. Typical of his verbal acrobatics is the label in *Norman the Doorman* for a driftwood sculpture on view in the art museum, which reads: "Skater, by I. C. Pond." While at work on *Dandelion*, Freeman took to signing his own name "Don de Lion" and "Dondelion."

Not every play on words was strictly for laughs. In a letter to his publisher commenting on his wildly fluctuating finances, Freeman rue-

fully observed: "When confusion reigns it pours!" Embedded within "Corduroy," a name he first jotted down years before he wrote the tender story that immortalized it, is the name of his son, Roy.

Freeman's depiction of Corduroy's Lisa and her mother as African-Americans was an unusual choice for the time. In many areas of American life, the 1960s was a decade of significant progress for the civil rights movement. But as educator Nancy Larrick made clear in a widely discussed article published in the September 11, 1965, issue of *Saturday Review*, America's publishers of children's books remained largely oblivious to social change. In "The All-White World of Children's Books," Larrick accused publishers of complicit racism for the narrowly selective portrait of American society they consistently offered in books for young people. Without fanfare, Freeman had apparently decided to do something to help right this wrong.

In a letter to the last of his Viking editors, Linda Zuckerman, Freeman cited two other inspirations for his most popular book. In creating *Corduroy*, he recalled, he had wanted "to do a story about a department store in which a character wanders around at night after the doors close . . . [and a] story to show the vast difference between the luxury of a department store [and] the simple life [most people live]."

Freeman recognized the role of America's sprawling postwar shopping emporia as dream theaters of material plenty. He understood that while admission to the show was free, only those with money could hope to go home singing the tunes. Readers come to one of the more piquant moments in the picture-book literature of the time with the unfettered exchange between Lisa, who begs her mother buy Corduroy for her, and the mother, who replies: "Not today, dear. . . . I've spent too much already."

If the African-American characterizations in Corduroy deserve our praise as the timely gesture of a person of conscience, Freeman's drawings of the Witch Doctor in *Tilly Witch* (1969) can remind readers of today that one era's comic characters

may well turn out to be another era's unacceptable stereotypes. Freeman doubtless intended to mine nothing other than a little good, slapstick fun from his drawings and mentions of the medical masked man. But much has changed since that time in our general awareness of cultural differences, and of the sensitivity toward others that those differences require. It is a point worth making with a child when reading this otherwise still very amusing tale of a witch gone soft on mischief and mayhem.

Looking back after Don Freeman's death at the artist's prints, drawings, and paintings of the 1930s and '40s, the theater critic John Beaumont was surprised to discover a thematic thread leading clearly to the picture books that followed. "It struck me," Beaumont wrote, "how frequently children figure in [them]. . . . Children race through the first outdoor art exhibit in Washington Square. They dance to coax coins from theatergoers at intermission time. They wait patiently, along with grown-up actors, to audition for a part in a play. They shine shoes, peddle newspapers, and join the

Times Square celebration of an FDR victory. . . . For a man who was to become an author and illustrator of children's books, the emphasis was appropriate, if not prophetic." As a picture book artist, Freeman had, in turn, found a way to keep his hand and heart in pictorial storytelling and in the theater. A performer by nature, in the late 1950s he became one of the first children's-book artists to take to the lecture circuit. Standing at an easel, Freeman joked with his young library story hour audiences while adroitly sketching characters and scenes from his books. Behind the banter lay the wish, as he once told a reporter, to "help in any way to encourage children to start reading and get them excited about books." By all accounts the effect was pure magic. It would have to have been to please Freeman himself. As the kindly prompter reminds Maestro Petrini, as a special children's matinee of *The Magic Flute* is about to begin: "We must be especially good today, my pet. Boys and girls deserve the very best, you know!"

—Leonard S. Marcus

Corduroy

• *1968* •

CORDUROY IS A BEAR WHO ONCE LIVED IN THE TOY DEPARTMENT OF A BIG STORE. Day after day he waited with all the other animals and dolls for somebody to come along and take him home.

The store was always filled with shoppers buying all sorts of things, but no one ever seemed to want a small bear in green overalls.

Then one morning a little girl stopped and looked straight into Corduroy's bright eyes.

"I didn't know I'd lost a button," he said to himself. "Tonight I'll go and see if I can find it."

Late that evening, when all the shoppers had gone and the doors were shut and locked, Corduroy climbed carefully down from his shelf and began searching every-where on the floor for his lost button.

"Oh, Mommy!" she said. "Look! There's the very bear I've always wanted."

"Not today, dear." Her mother sighed. "I've spent too much already. Besides he doesn't look new. He's lost the button to one of his shoulder straps."

Corduroy watched them sadly as they walked away.

Suddenly he felt the floor moving under him! Quite by accident he had stepped onto an escalator—and up he went!

"Could this be a mountain?" he wondered. "I think I've always wanted to climb a mountain."

He stepped off the escalator as it reached the next floor, and there, before his eyes, was a most amazing sight—tables and chairs and lamps and sofas, and rows and rows of beds.

"This must be a palace!" Corduroy gasped. "I guess I've always wanted to live in a palace."

He wandered around admiring the furniture.

"This must be a bed," he said. "I've always wanted to sleep in a bed." And up he crawled onto a large, thick mattress.

All at once he saw something small and round.

Corduroy didn't know it, but there was someone else awake in the store. The night watchman was going his rounds on the floor above. When he heard the crash he came dashing down the escalator.

"Now who in the world did that!" he exclaimed. "Somebody must be hiding around here!"

He flashed his light under and over sofas and beds until he came to the biggest bed of

"Why, here's my button!" he cried. And he tried to pick it up. But, like all the other buttons on the mattress, it was tied down tight.

He yanked and pulled with both paws until POP! Off came the button—and off the mattress Corduroy toppled, *bang* into a tall floor lamp. Over it fell with a crash!

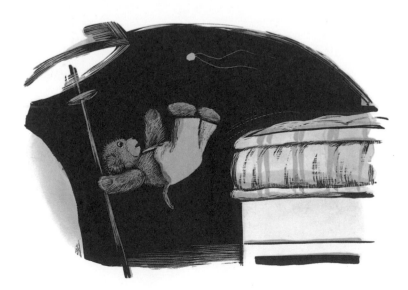

all. And there he saw two fuzzy brown ears sticking up from under the cover.

"Hello!" he said. "How did *you* get upstairs?"

The watchman tucked Corduroy under

his arm and carried him down the escalator and set him on the shelf in the toy department with the other animals and dolls.

Corduroy was just waking up when the first customers came into the store in the morning. And there, looking at him with a wide, warm smile, was the same little girl he'd seen only the day before.

"I'm Lisa," she said, "and you're going to be my very own bear. Last night I counted what I've saved in my piggy bank and my mother said I could bring you home."

"Shall I put him in a box for you?" the saleslady asked. "Oh, no thank you," Lisa answered. And she carried Corduroy home in her arms.

She ran all the way up four flights of stairs, into her family's apartment, and straight to her own room.

Corduroy blinked. There was a chair and a chest of drawers, and alongside a girl-size bed stood a little bed just the right size for him. The room was small, nothing like that enormous palace in the department store.

"This must be home," he said. "I *know* I've always wanted a home!"

Lisa sat down with Corduroy on her lap and began to sew a button on his overalls.

"I like you the way you are," she said, "but you'll be more comfortable with your shoulder strap fastened."

"You must be a friend," said Corduroy. "I've always wanted a friend."

"Me too!" said Lisa, and gave him a big hug.

To Sally Elizabeth Kildow and Patrick Steven Duff Kildow, who know how a bear feels about buttons—D. F.

Chuggy and the Blue Caboose

· 1951 ·

ONCE THERE WAS A LITTLE BLUE CABOOSE WHICH WAS HARDLY EVER IN USE. The reason this little caboose was blue was because long years before it had been used as an end-car to a gay circus train. One day however, this little caboose came loose from the rest of the gay circus train and was left standing alone on a side-track—near this busy railroad yard.

All the other cabooses in the busy railroad yard were painted Tuscan red. When they went past the little Blue Caboose they always turned up their noses.

And whenever these red cabooses got together on one track you could hear them gossiping. "Whoever heard of a caboose being blue!" they would whisper. "Look at us. We come from a long line of freight cars, and she comes from only a short circus train!"

But no matter what the red cabooses said or thought, the little Blue Caboose had at

least one good friend in the busy railroad yard, and this was Chuggy, the little engine who lived here in this roundhouse.

Chuggy felt lonely too, just the same as the little Blue Caboose, even though he was very much in use. He worked hard all night long, switching, hitching, pushing, and pulling freight cars, while the big engines were fast asleep inside the roundhouse.

To tell the truth, Chuggy had seen more service on the railroad than all the other engines put together. Once, years before, he had even been a snowplower high up in the Rocky Mountains. But the big engines like Loco Louie and Dan Diesel thought that Chuggy was old-fashioned and useless.

Each night when Chuggy went out into the yard to switch, hitch, push, and pull he would be sure to flash his headlight at the lonely little caboose over on the siding.

Then—one bright moonlight night something wonderful happened. What should he see across the yard but the little Blue Caboose all lit up for the first time! And when he turned his headlight on her she actually blinked back.

As you might expect, this made Chuggy feel so happy that he went chugging down the track lickety-split.

In a minute he was on the way to visit his old pal Mitch the Switchman, who kept a garden by his trackside shack. Chuggy wanted to ask Mitch why the caboose on the siding had all her lights lit.

"Oh, you mean Lucy the Blue Caboose!" said Mitch. "Well, sir, we switchmen are fixing her up to use as a sort of club car. We're putting in a stove, some chairs, and a table. They say it's going to be a pretty cold winter, and we may be needing a special place to keep warm."

Chuggy could hardly believe his gears, he was so happy. "Then will you do me a favor?" Chuggy steamed. "Please give Lucy a bouquet of your finest flowers for me." "Certainly!" said Mitch. "But I have only a few batchelor's-buttons and sunflowers left. It's rather late in the fall for flowers, you know, but I'll do my best!"

That morning when Chuggy went back to the roundhouse he slept sounder than he had for many a sun.

And see what Lucy looked like with flowers in her hat!

Now when the slick silver streamliner whizzed past every afternoon he hooted his horn at her rudely. "Woooooo-woooooo!" he hooted.

Not long afterward winter suddenly came, with fury and force and snowflakes. Just see what the first blizzard did to poor Lucy and her fancy bouquet!

Gradually the thick white snow began to cover everything in the whole railroad yard—

everything, even the Tuscan-red cabooses and their long lines of freight cars. The big strong locomotives, too, were stopped cold in their tracks.

This was the worst snowstorm the yard had ever known! But no matter how hard it snowed, one track had to be kept clear. That was the track on which the slick silver streamliner was due to come. Everybody worked to shovel away the snow.

All at once Mitch the Switchman called out, "Clear the track! Clear the track! Streamliner ahead!"

The streamliner came streaking along,

All the railroad workers ran to the rescue, but just as fast as they shoveled off the snow more snow piled up on top. The mighty streamliner was getting paler and paler by the minute and slowly disappearing.

The conductor of the stuck streamliner dug himself out and shouted at the engineers who belonged to the yard. "You men have got to get us out of here in a hurry!

pushing aside the walls of snow as he came, until—GLUG! He hit a snowbank twice as high as himself, and there he stayed, stuck fast. He could not budge.

"Help, help!" he cried.

We have never been late in our life, and we *must* be on time today. No excuses! You'll have to find some way to get us through!"

"But all our engines are frozen stiff," explained the yard captain. "There's absolutely nothing we can do until the snow stops!"

"Stops!" screamed the conductor. "This snow won't stop for days! You'd better do

something quick if you know what's good for you!"

Just then Lucy the Blue Caboose shook herself loose from a snowdrift and sneezed. "Get Chuggy! Get Chuggy! Get-choooo!"

All the other engines stayed behind and shivered as they watched Chuggy pull out of the roundhouse.

"She's right!" yelled Mitch the Switchman. "Our Lucy's right! Let's get Chuggy. He used to be a snowplower up in the Rockies!"

As a matter of fact, Chuggy was already set and rarin' to go at that very minute. His snowplow was hooked on and his furnace fired up.

There he goes! A nod from Lucy was all he needed. Nothing could stop him now!

Everybody ran to see brave Chuggy pitching and pushing away the snowdrifts. In a jiffy or two he had completely cleared the track and was face to face with the streamliner!

"Hooray! Hooray!"

Although the surprised streamliner felt a bit embarrassed about being saved by such a little old-fashioned out-of-date engine, he also tooted, "Hooray!" in gratitude.

Then away he whizzed, down the track and out of sight.

Back inside the roundhouse that night, after the snowstorm had stopped, the big engines crowded around Chuggy. Loco

secret—a secret his pal Mitch the Switchman had told him. It seems Mitch knew of a wonderful Happy-Go-Lucky circus that needed an engine and also a Blue Caboose!

So several nights later, just as soon as he could, Chuggy switched onto the siding and puffed the question to you-know-who. He asked Lucy if she cared to join a circus with him in the spring. And would she? She would!

Louie stepped forward and said, "Congratulations, Chuggy, my boy! Let me be the first to shake your fender!"

Outside in the cold yard, Lucy wondered if the switchmen had forgotten about her.

But of course they hadn't forgotten! Around midnight, when Chuggy came out, the switchmen were all inside the warm caboose. They celebrated by making up songs about how their Chuggy had saved the day for the whole railroad yard. But can you guess what Chuggy did?

He went right on with his work, hitching, switching, pushing, and pulling freight cars! And yet he went with a light heart and a

Finally the great day arrived. It was the first day of spring, and bright and early in the morning off they went to find the

Happy-Go-Lucky circus. Naturally Mitch came along to see that they got off on the right track!

After searching for many days, they found the gayest and Happy-Go-Luckiest circus train you ever did see. All the clowns and animals and acrobats welcomed them both as part of the family.

From town to town they all traveled, bringing fun and frolic to children everywhere. So no wonder they say that Chuggy and the Blue Caboose chugged on happily ever after.

The end.

Pet of the Met

· 1953 ·

HIGH UP IN THE ATTIC OF THE METRO-POLITAN OPERA HOUSE, IN A FORGOTTEN harp case, there once lived a white mouse named Maestro Petrini.

With him lived Madame Petrini and their three teeny-weeny Petrinis, Doe, Ray, and Mee.

Next to his family Maestro Petrini loved the opera more than anything else in the world. He knew all the opera stories by heart and could hum most of the music. This was not surprising because he worked for his daily cheese downstairs in the Opera House itself.

Here he is, working as a page turner for the Prompter, in the Prompter's box.

The Prompter's box is a small cavelike place set in the center of the stage footlights.

No one in the audience ever sees or hears the Prompter, but he is a very important man. The singers watch and listen to him, for they depend upon him to help them remember the words of their songs if they should ever forget.

The Prompter was always careful to keep Maestro Petrini well hidden behind the big music book, and for two good reasons: first, singers are not exactly partial to mice; and second, the Prompter knew of a certain cat, named Mefisto, who lived in the basement

just below. Mefisto lived
in an empty violin case,
but he hated music more than anything else
in the world, except mice.

Every time he heard singing from upstairs
he would try to shut out the sound. He
wouldn't even let himself listen to find out
whether or not he liked it. He was just plain
prejudiced against music.

Every night after the performance it was
his job to rid the great Opera House of
mice. This is how he earned his daily bowl
of milk. It was an easy job because he never
found any victims.

The Opera House was so enormous that
Mefisto had never discovered the attic high

at the top. This was fortunate for the
carefree Petrinis.

During his spare time Maestro Petrini
would put on his own opera performances
with his family as the cast. Of all the operas
their favorite was *The Magic Flute* by Mozart.

The Magic Flute is about a prince who,
with a magic flute to protect him, searches
for his princess throughout the realm of the
Queen of the Night. A funny birdcatcher
named Papageno helps him to find his way.
Whenever they are in danger the music
of the magic flute charms even the most
ferocious animals of the forest. This is how
they are able to make their way safely
through every
trial.

Maestro Petrini took great delight in playing the part of the foolish birdcatcher. Madame Petrini had made his costume out of an old feather duster she had found in the corner of the attic.

Madame Petrini herself preferred to play the Queen of the Night. She made her costume out of some dark-blue cheesecloth she just happened to have handy.

The scene they all liked best was the one in which the ferocious animals of the forest dance to the music of the magic flute. You can imagine who whistled like a flute!

For this scene Doe dressed up as a lion by wearing a mop and tying a tassel to the end of his tail. Ray became a rabbit by folding back his ears and tying his tail into a bunny-knot. As for Mee, he merely put on his mother's green spectacles and painted stripes around his tail. You couldn't tell him from a tiger!

They danced this scene so hard and so long that they never were able to finish the rest of the opera, no matter how early they had started.

One day just after an especially wonderful dancing scene, the teeny-weeny Petrinis gathered around their papa and breathlessly pleaded, "Please, Papa, when can we go downstairs and see you act in the real opera?"

That very evening as they sat down to an elegant cheese-soufflé supper, Papa Petrini gave his family a surprise and a promise. They would all be permitted to attend a Special Children's Opera matinee the next day. It was to be *The Magic Flute*!

First thing the next morning Madame Petrini set about washing everybody's ears. She wanted to make sure that not a single note would be missed!

Maestro Petrini combed his hair and curled his whiskers, a process which took most of the morning.

Meanwhile, downstairs, Mefisto, the cat,  suspected that something extraordinary was going on that afternoon. He went prowling around backstage, searching for you know who! When he peeked through the peephole in the curtain this is what he saw. The children were already beginning to arrive for the matinee!

Upstairs in the attic at this very moment the Petrinis were setting out, all primped and powdered and on their best behavior.

Maestro Petrini had to let his family find their own seats while he hurried off to his Prompter's box to get ready for the performance.

Soon every seat in the entire Opera House was filled. But where are Madame Petrini and Doe, Ray, Mee?

Here they are! They have found themselves a perfect place. What could be better than to snuggle behind a young lady's white gloves?

Gradually the lights all over the house dimmed down. Everyone was silent and expectant.

The orchestra conductor appeared and made one long deep bow.

Then the overture began.

Just before the great golden curtains parted, the Prompter leaned over and whispered into his partner's ear, "We must be especially good today, my pet. Boys and girls deserve the very best, you know!"

Then the curtain went up. The opera was under way!

When Papageno, the foolish birdcatcher, appeared and began to sing the audience was all eyes and ears.

And when the Prince played upon his flute, one by one the stage animals came out and danced to the magic music.

But look! Can it be? Yes, it is! Maestro

Petrini, completely carried away by the music, has leaped out of his box before the Prompter can stop him!

He's dancing! And what's more he is dancing in perfect rhythm to the music!

Of course none of the children in the audience can see the tiny Maestro dancing. But his family can. They are taking turns looking through a pair of opera glasses left resting on the velvet railing. And to tell the awful truth, someone else is watching! The cat, Mefisto! He watches from the dark side-curtains backstage!

like streaks of lightning, while the flute music grows more and more beautiful and exciting until poor Petrini is caught by his coat tail! But wait—

The strangest thing is happening. What can it be? Mefisto is suddenly beginning to feel and look different. He is falling under the spell of the flute music!

"Petrini! Run for your life!" shouts the Prompter.

Out springs Mefisto.

In and out about the stage Mefisto chases Petrini. Through the dancers' legs they speed

Now *he's* dancing! And dancing! Never in the history of the Metropolitan has there been such a scene—such waltzing and turning—such feline grace!

Even after the music had stopped Mefisto

place in the music book. You'll have to decide now, once and for all, whether you intend to be an opera star or a page-turner. You simply can't be both! I have a good notion to hire Mefisto the cat."

"Oh no, no!" pleaded Petrini. "I'll be your page-turner and I promise never to be an opera star again!"

That afternoon when the performance was over, a subdued and humbled Maestro returned to his home in the harp case. There, to his great surprise, his family showered him with bravos and squeals of applause! They told him his performance had been the best part of the opera!

and Petrini continued to whirl and twirl until the curtain had to be brought down.

When the audience called for more,

Maestro Petrini felt obliged to step out in front of the curtain and make several deep, dignified bows.

The Prompter reached out and pulled him back into the box. This broke the spell for Petrini.

The Prompter was very angry. "See here, my pet," he scolded, "you made me lose my

"And the cat was pretty funny, too!" said Doe. "The flute certainly tamed him down—and just in the nick of time!" To this remark Papa Petrini said nothing. He was hungry. And he had brought home a special present from his friend the Prompter—an extra-large portion of Swiss cheese!

Far down in the basement another opera lover was exhausted but happy. Mefisto, forgetting for the first time about ridding the

house of mice, had his supper and went straight to bed in his violin case. He purred himself to sleep with a tune from *The Magic Flute*.

As you might guess, Maestro Petrini and Mister Mefisto soon became good friends. And to this day it is said that between them they have the run of the entire Metropolitan Opera House!

Beady Bear

· 1954 ·

Then Thayer would always go find him and take his key and gently wind him.

Once Beady was all wound up, he wanted to keep on playing.

And yet when Thayer went to bed Beady knew he ought to, too.

One winter's day Thayer went away. Just when he'd be back he didn't say.

Being all alone for the first time Beady amused himself by looking at a book.

Beady was a fuzzy toy bear who belonged to a boy named Thayer.

Hide-and-seek was their favorite fun.

From time to time Beady would suddenly stop and topple over—kerplop! He'd come unwound!

B IS FOR BEAR
AN ANIMAL BRAVE
WHO LIVES
IN A CAVE.

"Why hasn't anybody told me this before?" said Beady sadly to himself.

"I wonder if there could be a cave for me away in those hills?"

Taking a long look through Thayer's shiny telescope he searched the side of the hill until—he spied a cave!

So he left a note.

Up the hill he climbed and climbed. At last!

He could hardly believe his beady eyes— it was just his size!

"A perfect place for a brave bear like me!" sighed Beady.

"And yet it's awfully dark and stilly here inside! And a wee bit chilly, really!"

That night Beady couldn't sleep a wink. "It's because of these sharp stones, I think.

"There's something I need in here to make me truly happy. I wonder what it could be?

"Oh, I know!" and up he got and out he trotted down the snowy hillside to his house far below.

And what should he bring back but his very own little pillow!

"This is more like it!" said Beady as he bedded down for the rest of the night.

"But there still seems to be something missing!"

So down the hill he trotted again and brought back—of all things—a flashlight.

But as soon as he settled down he knew there was something more a bear needed

to be truly happy. "What good is a light without something to read?" said Beady.

The evening papers, indeed!
Now what more could a bear ask for?

The noise grew louder and louder as Beady moved along, ever so slowly and shakily. Suddenly he came to a stop—and over he toppled—kerplop! "Who's there?" cried Beady, upside down.

"It's me, Thayer! I'm looking for my bear!"

But from inside the cave now came not a sound—Beady was much too embarrassed, lying there on the ground!

Well, after reading all the papers, Beady began to worry and wonder. "Maybe it's some toys I need . . ."

At this very moment he heard a loud noise outside. "It's a bear!" said Beady.

"I must be brave! This is probably his cave!"

"Well, hello, Beady boy! I thought I'd find you in this place. That's why I brought along your key, just in case!"

"Yes, but if I need you, who do you need?"

"I need Beady!"

So down the hill to home they went, paw in hand and hand in paw, and when Beady went to bed that night, he was the truly happiest bear you ever saw.

"For goodness' sakes, Beady don't you know you need a key?

"And me?"

For Marjorie Rankin of the Children's Room of the Santa Barbara Public Library—D. F.

Mop Top

· 1955 ·

roaring lion. A good lion he made too, without even trying!

But the time came when something had to be done about Moppy's top. And it happened one day when he was

swinging from branch to branch in his very own chinaberry tree.

His mother came out into the garden and said, "Pardon me, but just who do you think you are up there—Tarzan?"

"Oh no, Mother, I'm not Tarzan!" said Moppy. "I'm a man from Mars and I'm visiting all the stars and other planets!"

"Well then, Mister Man-from-Mars, could you plan to make a landing on this earth sometime today? We

THIS IS THE STORY OF A BOY WHO NEVER WANTED TO HAVE HIS HAIR CUT.

Everybody called him Moppy, because on top he looked like a floppy red mop.

Moppy didn't care what anybody said about his hair or what they called him. All he wanted was to stay at home and play.

He sometimes played at being a soaring eagle, and he sometimes played at being a

want you to hop to the barbershop and get that floppy mop clipped off before your birthday party tomorrow."

The minute Moppy heard the words "birthday party" he dropped down out of the tree to the ground, feet first, then stretched out his hand.

"Here's some money, sonny," his mother said. "I've just called Mister Barberoli, and he says he'll be ready for you at four o'clock sharp. It's a little after half-past three now, so let's see you hippity-hop to the barbershop all by yourself."

Moppy put the money in his pocket, and off he zoomed across the vacant lot, like a rocket to the moon.

But just as soon as he turned the corner he slowed down to a trot.

"Don't need my hair cut at all—anyway not now," he grumbled, and stumbled along

until some bright red lollipops in a candy-store window caught his eye. They looked so good he had to stop.

While he stood there staring, what should waddle up but a frilly woolly pup.

"What a silly-looking pup you are!" said Moppy as he bent down and tried to find

Mr. Lawson stopped to wipe his brow and said, "How about letting me use this machine on that grassy patch of yours, boy? It could do with a little mowing."

Moppy thought he ought to get going, so off he hopped.

But the closer he got to the barbershop, the slower he hopped.

He was nearly there when he saw a man on a ladder, snipping branches off a low, droopy tree.

"Maybe a tree needs a clipping, but not me!" said Moppy.

the pup's eyes. "You're the one who needs a haircut, not me!"

And then they both trotted away in opposite directions.

Moppy hadn't gone very far before he saw Mr. Lawson mowing his lawn.

"That lawn is what needs a haircut, not me!" said Moppy.

"Oh, I don't know about that," said the man on the ladder. "You could do with a few snips of these snippers, skipper!"

At that Moppy skipped away and came at last to the barbershop.

But hard as he tried, he could not go inside!

He decided to run and hide in the grocery store next door, where he could think things over.

And this is where he hid—behind a barrel of brooms and brushes and fancy red mops!

By and by a lady without her glasses came up and told the salesman she wanted

a mop to help her keep her kitchen floor clean.

"What's more, I want the strongest, fluffiest, floppiest mop you have in the store, sir," she said as she began shaking the mops, one at a time.

"Here, this one will do very well," said the lady. "I'll take it along with me right now."

"Ouch! Let go!" shouted Moppy. "I'm not a mop! I'm a boy!"

The lady certainly did let go, and in a hurry too, as Moppy scurried out the door and headed straight for Mister Barberoli's barbershop!

"I thought maybe you forgot," said roly-poly Mister Barberoli. "But you're right on the dot. It's exactly four!" Then in one long leap Moppy was up on the barber-chair seat ready to get his hair cut nice and neat.

"Please, Mister Barberoli, don't let me look like a mop any more," pleaded Moppy. "I don't want to clean anybody's kitchen floor!"

In a jiffy Mister Barberoli was clipping and snipping away, and combing and cropping without once stopping, as if he hadn't a minute to lose.

Finally he did stop. He held up a mirror and said, "Well, sonny, who's that, would you say?"

"It's me! It's me without that floppy old mop on top! Hooray!" said the boy in the chair.

Then he hopped down and gave Mister Barberoli the money. And out the door he flew, light as a feather.

All the world looked spick-and-span, as the boy who was once called Moppy hopped up the street for home.

Everything felt new now, even the weather! The tree was neat and tidy. The lawn was nicely mowed. And look at the pup! Even he's had a trim!

Which was his real and true name all the time and forevermore!

Next day at his Birthday Party there was a beautiful big cake with six candles lit, and on the frosting was written:

HAPPY BIRTHDAY TO MARTY!

For Chipper and Daryl, Michael and Diane, Ethan and Sean, Jeff and Roy, and all red-haired topknotters everywhere—D. F.

Fly High Fly Low

• *1957* •

IN THE BEAUTIFUL CITY OF SAN FRANCISCO, A CITY FAMOUS FOR ITS fogs and flowers, cable cars and towers, there once stood an electric-light sign on top of a tall building, and inside the letter B of this sign there lived a pigeon.

Before choosing to make his home here this proud gray pigeon had tried living in many other letters in the alphabet. Just why he liked the lower loop of the letter B, no one yet knew.

During the day the wide side walls kept the wind away, and at night the bright lights kept him warm and cozy.

The pigeons who roosted along the ledges of the building across the street thought he was a pretty persnickety pigeon to live where he did. "He's too choosy! He's too choosy!" they would coo.

The only one who never made fun of him was a white-feathered dove. She felt sure he must have a good reason for wanting to live in that letter.

Every morning as soon as the sun came up, these two met in mid-air and together they swerved and swooped down into Union Square Park, where they pecked up their breakfast. Mr. Hi Lee was certain to be there, throwing out crumbs from his large paper

sack. He would always greet them by saying, "Good morning, Sid and Midge. How are my two early birds?"

All the birds in the city regarded Mr. Hi Lee as their best friend, and he had nicknames for many of them. Sometime he brought them hard breadcrumbs and sometimes, as an extra-special treat, day-old cake crumbs from a nearby bakery.

After every crumb was pecked up, the pigeons always circled around Mr. Hi Lee's head, flapping their wings as they flew—which was their way of saying, "Thank you!"

By noontime Sid and Midge could be seen sailing high in the sky, flying into one cloud and out the other. Side by side they glided over the bay, until they could look down and see the Golden Gate Bridge.

Sid would swoop and fly through the open arches just to show Midge what a good looper he was.

Then, as the setting sun began painting the sky with a rosy glow, two tuckered out birds would be slowly winging their way back to the pack just in time for supper.

One evening after an especially gay lark in the sky, Sid invited Midge to stay and share his letter B with him.

Across the way pigeons were soon bobbing their heads up and down and cooing, "Whoever heard of birds building a nest in a sign? It'll never do! It'll never do!"

But Sid and Midge went right on building their nest as best they could. They used patches of cloth and strands of string and bits of straw, and gradually there grew a strong nest with a perfect view.

Then one misty morning a few weeks later, just as everything was going along smoothly, something happened which was very upsetting! It occurred right after Sid had flown down to the park to peck up his breakfast. As usual he had left Midge taking her turn sitting on the nest, where there were now two eggs to be kept warm!

Suddenly, like a bolt out of the blue, Midge felt their perch give a terrible lurch! The buildings across the way seemed to sway back and forth. "It's an earthquake!" screeched Midge.

But no—it was even worse than an earthquake! Their sign was being taken down! One by one the letters were being lowered into a waiting truck below. Midge followed, flapping her wings wildly at the movers, trying to let them know they must not take away her nest!

But the men paid no attention to her, until the tallest man stopped and shouted, "Hold everything! Look here what I've found! Two eggs in a nest! No wonder that pigeon has been making such a fuss!"

"Well, what do you know!" exclaimed another man as he took a peek inside. "We'll sure have to take good care of this letter. Come to think of it, I know of a bakery shop that could use a

big letter 'B.' Anyway, we won't be throwing this one away. Come on men, let's get going!"

Down the hill they went, and far out of sight, with Midge clinging on with all her might!

You can imagine how Sid felt when he landed back on the cold and empty scaffold later that morning! He stood there dazed

and bewildered, wondering where his sign had gone. Where was his Midge? And where, oh where, was their nest with those two precious eggs?

He looked around on all sides, but not a

trace of his sign did he see. Suddenly off he flew.

First to the waterfront. Possibly the sign was being loaded onto a boat. Sid was sure that wherever that particular letter 'B' was, there, too, Midge would be. He looked high and he looked low, but not a sign of his letter did he spy.

Next he flew to the uppermost post of the Golden Gate Bridge. He thought perhaps Midge might have passed by that way. But no, not a feather did he find.

While he stood wondering where to search next, an enormous fog bank came rolling in from off the ocean. Like a rampaging flock of sheep, the fog came surging straight toward him!

When Sid saw this he puffed out his chest and stretched his wings wide and cried, "Who's afraid of a little breeze? I'll flap my wings and blow the wind away!"

But the fog rolled silently on, and before Sid knew what had happened he was completely surrounded by a dense, damp grayness. And the faster he flew, the thicker the fog grew, until he could barely see

beyond his beak. Down, down he dived, hoping to land on solid ground.

All at once he found himself standing on top of a traffic-light signal right in the busiest part of town!

Once inside the green "Go" signal, Sid began fluffing up his wings, trying to dry them off before going on with his search for Midge.

What Sid didn't know was that his fluffed-up wings hid the word "Go," and no one in the street dared to budge. Soon there was a roar of automobile horns! "People certainly get awfully upset over a little fog!" said Sid as he stuck out his head.

Just then along came a policeman, and when he blew his whistle—BEEEP!

BEEEP!—Sid flew out

like a streak of lightning! At last the traffic could move on!

By now the fog had changed to rain and everybody started hopping aboard the cable cars—which is what people do in San Francisco wherever the hills are too steep or the weather is too wet.

And that's exactly what Sid did! Under the big bell on top of the cable car he found a perfect umbrella.

If only the conductor hadn't shouted, "Hold on tight! Sharp corner ahead!" and then clanged the bell! The clapper of the bell hit Sid so hard that he fell overboard.

In the street gutter below, all bruised and weary, he hobbled along, muttering to himself, "People! It's all people's fault!"

But then he began to think of

the kind man in the park. Would Mr. Hi Lee be there on such a terrible day as this? Sid tried to spread his wings and fly, but he was too weak. He would have to walk all the way to Union Square.

Fortunately the park was only a couple of blocks away, and just as Sid hopped up onto the curb he felt a gentle hand reach down and pick him up.

The next thing Sid knew he was inside Mr. Hi Lee's warm overcoat pocket, where, much to his surprise, he found several sunflower seeds. Right away he began to feel better. He could hardly wait to get on with his search for Midge.

When he peeped out, he saw that the rain had stopped and warm rays from the sun were beginning to shine down. Mr. Hi Lee talked to his friend inside his pocket as he walked along. "Around the corner from here I know of a bakery where we can get something more for you to eat," he said.

As they neared the shop Mr. Hi Lee noticed some men putting a large letter in the sign above the doorway. "Well, look at that—a new letter B!"

Out popped Sid's head, farther. What was

that he heard? It sounded exactly like a certain bird he knew cooing. Could it be?

Yes indeed! It was his very own Midge! She had stayed with their nest through thick and thin.

Up flew Sid like an arrow shot from a bow. And oh, what a meeting! Such billing and cooing as you've never heard! And no wonder, for their two eggs were just about to hatch!

head flapping his wings happily. And we know what he meant by that!

Some time later, when their old neighbors came flying by, they saw Sid and Midge peacefully perched in the lower loop of the letter B and the two little ones in the upper loop. "Oh those lucky birds!" they cooed as they flew away. "Sid certainly did know what he was doing when he chose that letter B!"

Out came two tiny beaks breaking through their shells!

And out of the bakery shop came the baker and his customers. They all wanted to know what the excitement was about.

Sid knew that his first duty was to find some food for Midge, so down he flew, and there was Mr. Hi Lee already holding out his hand full of cake crumbs!

After taking the crumbs to Midge, Sid hurried right back down, and this time he circled around and around Mr. Hi Lee's

This story is for YOU and for Ronnie and Laurie, Charlene and Bruce, Marc and Archy, Joan and Mary Jo, with a nudge to Mudge and Judy—D. F.

Norman the Doorman

· 1959 ·

IN FRONT OF A SMALL, WELL-HIDDEN HOLE AROUND
IN BACK OF THE MAJESTIC MUSEUM OF ART THERE
once stood a mouse named Norman.

Norman was a doorman, and he greeted all the
art-loving creatures who came to see the treasures
which were kept in the basement of the museum.

"Come right in!" Norman would say to his cousins the Petrinis. "We're quite safe. I've sprung all the traps."

Norman would explain every painting in detail and handle each masterpiece with as much care and respect as if he had painted it himself!

He would also take great pride in pointing out the artistic features of certain pieces of Greek sculpture which rested in the dark corners of the storage room.

Norman's only worry was keeping out of sight of the sharp-eyed guard, who often came to the basement to set traps for mice!

His bright flash-light frightened the

visitors, and they dashed out the secret hole into the night like streaks of pink and white lightning.

As for Norman, he always managed to escape and hide inside an old armored knight's helmet. Up there he felt perfectly safe.

Actually the helmet was Norman's home, which he had made into a very comfortable and workable studio. Just see what a splendid skylight the visor made!

Like most everybody, Norman had a hobby. Each night after work he tried to create something pleasing or beautiful—perhaps a painting of Swiss cheese and crackers, or a statue.

One bitter cold day Norman decided to stay in his studio and make something out of wire. For some time he had been collecting mousetraps and odd scraps of picture-hanging wire, with the intention of putting them to artistic use.

The mousetraps weren't any good any more, since Norman had cleverly taken out the pieces of cheese and then snapped the traps shut without having harmed even so much as a whisker on his nose.

All through the day and far into the night Norman twisted and bent wires into many strange and mysterious shapes—until, at last, he created something he was really proud of! It looked for all the world like a mouse on a trapeze.

That night when he finally went to sleep he was a tired but very happy mouse.

Early next morning when Norman went outside to shovel away the snow in front of his doorway he noticed a man reading a sign nearby.

He too read the sign— Back he flew!

SCULPTURE CONTEST
OPEN TO ALL ARTISTS, GREAT AND SMALL!

PRIZES! PRIZES!

WORKS IN STONE, IRON, BRONZE, WOOD, OR WIRE WELCOME

LAST DAY TODAY!

"Why can't I show my wire statue?" he said as he slid through the visor-lid opening.

But what would he call it? All pieces must have titles, he well knew.

Suddenly he had an inspiration. Stripping off the printed word "TRAP" from the label, and then ripping off the letters "EESE" from the word "cheese," he pasted them together.

Now he had a fitting title for his wire work! Although Norman was a modest mouse, he practically burst a button off his coat.

Then, as this was the last day for the artists to bring their sculpture pieces in, Norman put a cover over his statue, as he had seen the others do, and away he scooted.

Up the front stairway he climbed, one snowy step at a time.

Once inside the huge museum, he eagerly followed the other sculptors from one room to another. He still had to be extremely careful of the sharp-eyed guard! Contest or not, he didn't want to get caught!

After carefully removing the cover from his wire statue, he left it on the floor with the rest of the contestants' work.

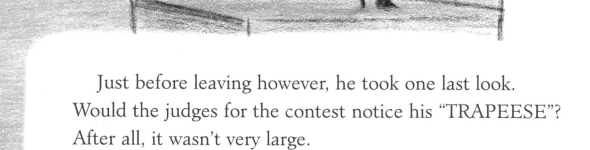

Just before leaving however, he took one last look. Would the judges for the contest notice his "TRAPEESE"? After all, it wasn't very large.

Out he went into the snowy afternoon knowing he had done his best.

Back once more in his helmet studio, Norman went about sewing new brass buttons on his blue coat. You see, he had not forgotten that he was a doorman who had a job to do.

Meanwhile, upstairs in the Sculpture Gallery of the

museum, the judges were busy judging. Quietly and seriously they examined each piece, trying to find which ones deserved prizes.

Gradually they found themselves huddled around a certain statue.

"Now *this* is an amazing creation!" exclaimed one of the judges.

"There's no name," said another. "And isn't it a shame it's so tiny!"

"Yes, but remember the contest is open to great and small," said another judge.

One by one each guard, when asked if he knew who had brought it in, shook his head and said, "No, not I." The Museum director couldn't understand why none of them had caught sight of the artist.

But when the sharp-eyed guard took a closer look he gasped. "Oh, so this is where all my mousetraps have been going! I think I know where to start searching for the tricky trap-snatcher!"

Without waiting another minute, the guard snapped on his flashlight and hurried downstairs to the basement.

"What's this—one of my traps stuck in a knight's helmet?"

He lifted up the visor to investigate. There inside he saw pieces of wire and parts of traps and—strangest of all—a neat straw bed which could only belong to a mouse.

"Whoever he is, he must be mighty fond of my cheese," said the guard as he knelt down on the floor and pointed the flashlight at some tracks which led out through the hole in the wall.

During all this time Norman had been tending to his duty as doorman. A party of

mice from the country, for whom he had been waiting, was long past due, and he was getting mighty cold and hungry.

But to his surprise, who should be coming around the corner but the sharp-eyed guard!

"Oho, so there you are!" said the guard as Norman fled inside.

But when the guard held a piece of cheese just above the hole and Norman sniffed it, he couldn't help poking his nose out to get a better whiff.

And just as he was about to reach up and snatch the cheese, a hand came down swiftly and caught Norman by his tail!

"Say, are you the rascal who's been taking my mousetraps every day and using them for artistic purposes?" asked the guard sternly.

"It's just a hobby!" sobbed Norman. "Just my hobby!"

Right then and there the guard tossed Norman up on his shoulders, but he still kept a tight hold on his tail. Norman was sure he was being taken to jail.

You can imagine his surprise when, instead, they entered the museum and heard the artists all clapping and cheering. "Hooray for 'Trapeese'!" they shouted. "Hooray for 'Trapeese'!"

"Well, I'll be bamboozled!" cried the guard. "I do believe you've won a prize! And

they're waiting for you to step forward and receive the award!"

The guard rushed up to the judges' platform and said proudly, "Here's the winner! I found him freezing outdoors in the snow!"

"Oh, indeed!" said the head judge, somewhat flustered. "Why, yes—who else could have created the 'daring young mouse on the flying trapeze'? What is your name, my good fellow, and what would you like for your prize?"

"If you please, sir, my name is Norman. I'm the doorman downstairs, and I've always dreamed of seeing the upstairs part of the museum without getting caught. That is what I would like best."

This simple request was granted immediately. Amidst great applause, the guard led Norman out into the Hall, where together they began a grand tour of the entire art museum!

Later that night when Norman returned to his door downstairs he found his mice friends from the country waiting for him there. Of course Norman invited them into his studio, where he shared with them an enormous slice of Cheddar cheese—a present given him by the kindhearted guard. Oh, what a wonderful way to end the day!

Good Knight!

To Doyle and David, Hilary and Tony, Wiggy and Tuni, Stevie and Sarah, Bernard and Curtis, and with two pieces of cheese for my nieces, Donna and Patti—D. F.

Dandelion

· 1964 ·

ON A SUNNY SATURDAY MORNING DANDELION WOKE UP, STRETCHED AND yawned, and jumped out of bed.

After doing his daily exercises Dandelion looked out of the window, blinked his eyes, and said, "I wonder if the mail has come?"

He put on his sweater and went outside to the mailbox. There was a letter, and it was written in fancy gold ink!

Dear Dandelion:
You are invited to my tea-and-taffy party on Saturday afternoon at half-past three.
Come as you are.
Sincerely,
Jennifer Giraffe

Dandelion was very excited. "Why, that's today!" he said. "It's a good thing I planned to get a haircut!"

As soon as he had washed and dried the breakfast dishes and made his bed nice and neat, he ran down the street to the barbershop.

Lou Kangaroo had a chair waiting for him. First he trimmed Dandelion's hair, and then gave him a shampoo.

Dandelion thought he should have a manicure too.

When Lou Kangaroo had finished Dandelion looked a bit foolish. His mane was frizzy and fuzzy and completely unrulish.

"Maybe a wave would help," Lou suggested, showing him a picture in the latest fashion magazine for lions.

Dandelion agreed. This was exactly what he needed.

So Lou went about curling his mane.

He looked magnificent!

But now Dandelion thought he really should wear something more elegant than a sweater to the party.

"This jacket is the very newest style," said Theodore the Tailor, "and it just fits you. All you need now is a cap and a cane.

Happy Crane will be glad to help you."

What a dapper dandy he had suddenly become!

"It's nearly half-past three!" said Dandelion. "I've just time to get something for my hostess!"

A bouquet of dandelions would be perfect.

He knew this tall door very well, having been here many times before.

He rang the bell.

When Jennifer Giraffe opened the door she looked very surprised. "Yes?" she said. "What can I do for you?"

"Why, I've come to your party," he answered.

"Oh, I'm sorry, sir, but you are not anyone I know!" said Miss Giraffe. "You must have come to the wrong address."

And with this she closed the door right in poor Dandelion's face!

"I'm Dandelion!" he roared. "You've made a mighty mistake!" But there was no use knocking. The door stayed tight shut.

Dandelion began walking back and forth. Back and forth, up and down the long block he paced.

And as he paced, the sky grew dark. Then a sudden gust of wind sprang up and blew away his beautiful bouquet, and his snappy cap flew off!

To make matters worse, it began to rain in torrents. Dandelion dropped his cane and stood under a weeping willow tree.

But the rain poured down through the branches. Dandelion was soon soaking wet and his curls came unfurled.

He took off his jacket and hung it on a willow branch. Luckily he had kept on his sweater.

At last the rain stopped and the warm sunshine came beaming down.

Dandelion decided to sit on Jennifer Giraffe's front steps until his mane was dry.

While he sat there waiting he spied three dandelion flowers under the bottom step where they had been protected from the wind and the rain.

He picked the dandelions and said, "I think I will try again."

And he rang the bell.

"Well, well! If it isn't our friend Dandelion at last!" said Jennifer Giraffe. "We've been waiting for you for the past hour. I do hope you weren't caught in that awful cloudburst!"

Everyone at the party greeted him heartily.

Later on when all her guests were enjoying tea and taffy, Jennifer Giraffe told Dandelion about the silly-looking lion who had come to the door earlier.

Dandelion almost spilled his cup of tea as he reared back and laughed uproariously, "Oh, that was me! I was that silly-looking lion!"

Miss Giraffe was so flustered she got herself all tangled up in her long pearl necklace. "I do apologize for having closed the door on you!" she said blushing. "I promise never to do such a thing again!"

"And I promise you I will never again try to turn myself into a stylish dandy," said Dandelion as he sipped his tea. "From now on I'll always be just plain me!"

To Lucas Lackner—D. F.

Tilly Witch

· 1969 ·

ONE BRIGHT MOONLIT NIGHT, TILLY IPSWITCH, QUEEN OF HALLOWEEN, stood atop her high mountain peak and sighed, "My, my! What a lovely evening! It makes me feel like being kind to everyone in the world, especially children."

For a wicked witch to have such kindly feelings was, to say the least, quite a switch!

Here it was, nearly Halloween, and Tilly was acting as if she were Queen of the May. Her pet cat, Kit, hid behind a rock and yowled, "Mee-ow! Mee-ouch!"

"Now, Kit," said Tilly, "if boys and girls can have fun pretending to be witches, I don't see why I can't play at being happy and gay, just for a change!"

But later, when Tilly tried to switch back to being a wicked witch again, she couldn't!

She ran inside her house and looked in the mirror. "That's queer!" she said, giggling, "I don't look a bit like my mean old self.

Now, how can I frighten children when I feel so good?"

Something certainly had to be done about this, and in a hurry!

Tilly spread out a map on the floor. "Maybe I ought to go see a witch doctor," she told Kit. "I've heard of a Doctor Weegee who lives on this tiny island called Wahoo. They say he cures witches without taking stitches."

Tilly put on a purple dress and dashed down to her broomport where she kept her new flyer: a surfboard with a whisk broom for a skeg.

see Tilly in such a giddy mood, Doctor Weegee was horrified.

"Ah Wahee! Ah Hogwash!" he bellowed, which in Wahooese means, "You happy witch! You are very bad!"

Once inside his hut the doctor examined Tilly from the tip of her hat to the tips of her slippers. Finally, he handed her a card on which was written this prescription: MISS FITCH'S FINISHING SCHOOL FOR WITCHES.

"Take good care of the bats and owls, Kit!" she shouted as she sailed into the sky. "I'll be back when I feel worse!"

With the skill of a seasoned surf rider, Tilly rode the crest of the billowy clouds, singing as she streaked along. At last she sighted the small island of Wahoo far below.

After making a happy landing, Tilly danced along to the door of the witch doctor's hut. But instead of being pleased to

Tilly hardly needed to be told what this meant. She had to go back to school, the same school she had attended many years before!

Hopping aboard her surfbroom, she waved a cheery "good-by" and away she flew.

You can imagine Miss Fitch's surprise when she opened the gate and beheld Tilly Ipswitch, her former prize pupil, standing there, *smiling*.

Without saying so much as, "How voodoo you do," Miss Fitch led Tilly straight to a classroom where students were busily carving out fierce-looking faces in pumpkins.

Tilly tried her best to be serious but even

during the class in Black Magic she simply could not keep from giggling.

Naturally Miss Fitch was furious, but no matter how much she scolded, Tilly still felt frivolous.

At cooking class that evening, Tilly behaved worse than ever. The student witches were learning how to mix a witch's brew, and each one was taking a turn at adding nasty-tasting things to the pot.

When it came Tilly's turn to show what she could do, she began pouring in syrup and sugar and instant chocolate pudding.

Miss Fitch shrieked. "Go to the corner this minute! And sit facing the wall!"

Poor Tilly was really in disgrace. And as if this weren't punishment enough, she had to wear a tall dunce hat!

For almost an hour, Tilly sat and

glowered at the blackboard. Then she began to think about scaring boys and girls. But who would be frightened by a happy witch? They would only *laugh* at her, or even worse, they might stop believing in Halloween!

The more Tilly thought of this the madder she got and the madder she got the meaner

she felt until suddenly she spun around, leaped off her stool and started stomping on the dunce hat. "I'm not a dunce!" she

screamed, "I'm Queen of Halloween, and I have important duties to attend to!"

Racing outside, she hopped aboard her surfbroom. Miss Fitch leaned out the window as Tilly sailed away. "Congratulations, Tilly!" she called. "I knew you'd remember your duty. You're the best student I've ever had!"

Heading straight for home, Tilly stopped only long enough to pick up a ripe pumpkin from her own pumpkin patch.

As soon as she landed on her mountain

peak, she quickly carved out a ferocious-looking face in the pumpkin. Then, placing it over her head, she crept silently up to her house and slowly opened the creaky door. . . .

"Trick or treat!" she screamed at the top of her lusty lungs. Poor Kit nearly hit the ceiling!

"Come down, my pet," Tilly coaxed. "See, it's really me, Tilly. I'm ready for Halloween. Come down—we have work to do tonight!"

And so, just about midnight, Tilly and Kit swept across the moonlit sky, riding astride their trusty old broomstick, scaring children everywhere. For Tilly had indeed learned her lesson. As long as Halloween comes once a year you can count on her to be the meanest and wickedest witch in all Witchdom.

To Susie and to Billy—D. F.

Flash the Dash

· 1973 ·

IN THE SMALL TOWN OF ROCKSUN THERE ONCE LIVED TWO DACHSHUNDS. Although they looked somewhat alike, Flash and Sashay were not alike in many ways.

They lived together in a neat, low-slung bungalow in the backyard of an empty house at sixteen sixty Bixby Street.

Flash was the lazy one. Instead of going out each day to earn their daily bone, he took long naps.

Sashay ran errands all around the town, delivering newspapers and flowers. In return she was always given a bone or a liverwurst sandwich to take home.

One morning Sashay decided the time had come for Flash to do his share. "Today it's your turn to go out there and help earn our living," she said sternly.

Flash had been dreading this moment but he rose to his feet and went down the street to look for steady employment.

Block after block he searched for work. But even though everyone in town knew Flash, no one seemed to have any work for him to do.

Just as he was about to give up, he saw a sign in the window of the Telegraph Office.

In he waddled, full of confidence and charm.

He took down the sign and held it in his mouth.

"Well, well! I'll be bamboozled!" said Mister Orkin, the telegraph operator. "It's Flash asking for work. Fancy that! I've got a good mind to take a chance on you."

After giving Flash a messenger's cap to wear, Mister Orkin said, "There! You're hired! Here's an important telegram that just came in over the wire. It's for the Mayor.

Now, let's see you get a wiggle on!"

Flash waggled his tail and out the door he rushed.

Since he knew everyone in Rocksun and everyone knew him, Flash hardly needed to ask for directions.

Up the steep steps of the City Hall he leapt—not an easy thing for such a young underslung dachshund!

Down the corridor he ran and into the Mayor's office he raced. He delivered the telegram to the Mayor's busy secretary.

Then out the door he tore and headed back to the Telegraph Office.

"Peapods and pickles!" exclaimed Mister Orkin. "That was fast! From now on I'm going to call you Flash the Dash!"

So, all that fall and on into winter Flash the Dash delivered telegrams to people in every part of Rocksun. As for pay, Mister Orkin gave him pretzels and sausages to take home to Sashay.

Sashay was amazed and surprised to see Flash dash out the door each morning as soon as the sun came up.

Some mornings he arrived at the Telegraph Office ahead of Mister Orkin. And when this happened Flash would do a few limbering-up exercises. Of course push-ups were easy for him to do because he didn't have far to push up.

These exercises kept him in good shape. He needed to keep fit, especially when it came to trudging through the winter snow.

Through blinding blizzards and hailstorms Flash never failed to perform his duties.

Day after day and night after night he delivered his messages. There were nights when he was so tired he would crawl into an old crate to sleep, even though he was far from home. Sashay never worried. She knew her mate would come home sooner or later.

But when spring came to the town of Rocksun, Flash began to get lazy again. Maybe he had a touch of spring fever. One day he spent the whole morning lying in a field of daisies, watching the clouds roll by in the sky. No one, not even Sashay or Mister Orkin knew where he was.

That same afternoon when he finally

arrived at the Telegraph Office, he found a telegram placed under the door.

Without looking to see to whom the telegram was addressed, Flash decided he needed a short rest before delivering it. So he sauntered over to the park.

He just couldn't see why anyone needed a telegram on such a lovely day. *Nothing* could possibly be all *that* important! He leaned against a tree and took a nap.

One look at the name and address and the lady knew who it was for . . .

"Flash! Flash!" she called. "Wake up! This telegram is for *you*!"

Flash sprang to his feet, stood on his hind legs and begged. The friendly lady understood what he meant. Opening the envelope, she began to read the message aloud . . .

While he snoozed, a sudden breeze swept through the trees and blew the telegram away.

Luckily, a friendly lady caught the telegram inside her parasol just before it fell into the lily pond!

WESTERN YOONYUN
Telegram

To FLASH THE DASH
1660 BIXBY STREET
CONGRATULATIONS. YOU ARE
THE FATHER OF THREE HEALTHY
PUPS. SASHAY DOING WELL AT
HOT DIGGETY DOG HOSPITAL.
TAKE DAY OFF. YOUR FRIEND
ORVILLE ORKIN

Without so much as a thank-you bark, Flash flew across the park.

Straight to the hospital he sped.

There, inside the maternity ward, he beheld the happiest sight of his life—three one-day-old puppies snuggled up to their mother. Needless to say, Sashay was very pleased to see their father. "You've been so busy lately, how did you ever know we were here, my dear?" she asked, all starry-eyed.

"Oh, I got the message!" replied Flash, blushing with pride. "I got the message!"

To Annie, Andrea, and Ari—D. F.

Gayelord

· *Unpublished* ·

Every morning farmer Mac Duff would set out
wheat and oats and other things he knew his goat liked to eat.

But there was something he didn't know,—

He soon came upon an artist painting a picture of a barn.
Of course Gaylord didn't know anything about Art but he did
know what he liked — bright colors!

Suddenly, he could resist no longer.

What a treat!
Colors began squishing out in every which direction.

and he pounced on one tube after another. Splish! Splash!

The following story was never published. Don Freeman submitted the book dummy (the sketches with rough text in place shown here) to May Massee, but she declined to publish it. Although the book was never finished, this look at a work in progress gives us a chance to see Don Freeman's creative process.

Gayelord is based on something that happened while Don and Lydia Freeman were staying with their good friend Harry Wickey (one of Don's former teachers) in Connecticut. Lydia was outside painting next to a fenced meadow that contained a goat. When Lydia came back from a lunch break, some of the color from her palette was gone and the goat was standing next to it, licking its mouth. Don and Lydia's son, Roy, recalls that Lydia used to love to tell the story of the goat who ate her paint.

GAYELORD WAS A FRISKY YOUNG GOAT WHO THOUGHT THE WORLD WAS MADE just for him to frolic in and to enjoy.

Every morning farmer Mac Duff would set out wheat and oats and other things he knew his goat liked to eat.

But there was something he didn't know,— Gayelord was also fond of nibbling on such things as toothpaste tubes and bright colored labels on tin cans. He relished the taste of paste but these delicacies weren't easy to find.

One day he went exploring for more taste sensations.

He soon came upon an artist painting a picture of a barn.

Of course Gayelord didn't know anything about Art but he did know what he liked— bright colors!

The artist, Miz Phipps, decided to have her picnic lunch by a stream not far away.

Gayelord was tempted to nibble on the colorful tubes of paint she had left behind.

He moved closer and closer.

Suddenly he could resist no longer. What a treat!

Colors began squishing out in every which direction.

In ecstasy he rolled on the paint-spattered grass and he pounced on one tube after another. Splish! Splash!

When Miz Phipps came back she almost

Of course Gayelord didn't understand one thing she was saying.

Weren't colors for having fun?

"He ought to be tied up and I'm going to find who
that goat belongs to, if it takes me all summer long!"

Miz Phipps went off in a sniff

flipped. "Oh, you bad goat, you've ruined my painting and squashed all my precious water-color tubes!"

Of course Gayelord didn't understand one thing she was saying. Weren't colors for having fun?

"He ought to be tied up and I'm going to find who that goat belongs to, if it takes me all summer long!"

Miz Phipps went off in a sniff while Gayelord returned to his hut on the hillside where he stayed the rest of the day and all that night. He wondered what he had done wrong.

Early the next morning when a few neigh-

bors passed by and saw Gayelord standing there in a blaze of colors, they were amazed.

"It's a miracle, that's what it is!" one of them said.

"We must tell our friends in the village," said still another neighbor.

Miz Phipps also happened to be passing by at the same time. "That's the goat who chewed up all my precious paint tubes and spoiled my beautiful painting!" she scolded. "Now you've got to do something about paying me back."

Poor farmer Mac Duff didn't know what he could possibly do. He hardly had a cent to spare. But later that afternoon as soon as

while Gaylord returned to his hut on the hillside where he stayed the rest of the day and all that night, he wondered what he had done wrong.

Early the next morning when a few neighbors passed by and saw Gaylord standing there in a blaze of colors, they were amazed.
" It's a miracle , that's what it is!" one of them said.
"We must tell our friends in the village." said still another neighbor.

Miz Phipps also happened to be passing by at the same time. "That's the goat who chewed up all my precious paint tubes and spoiled my beautiful painting!" she scolded. " Now you've got to do something about paying me back."

Poor farmer Mac Duff didn't know what he could possibly do. He hardly had a cent to spare. But later that same afternoon

There were so many people all wanting to take photographs, Mac Duff decided to hang up a banner. Miz Phipps helped him by charging admission at the gate.

He yanked and pulled, and pulled and yanked until finally,
the stake came loose!

Free once again!

Gayelord remembered a stream near a waterfall where he could
go for a dip. He didn't like all those silly people making fun
of the way he looked
So, in he slipped, horns first.

For an hour or more he enjoyed himself *swimming about under*
the waterfall.

the word spread to the village, crowds of people began to come. In busses and vans and on bicycles they came.

There were so many people all wanting to take photographs, Mac Duff decided to hang up a banner. Miz Phipps helped him by charging admission at the gate.

That evening after the crowds had dispersed, Mac Duff tied Gayelord to a stake. He certainly didn't want his valuable goat to go wandering away!

But Gayelord didn't like this one bit.

He yanked and pulled, and pulled and yanked until finally, the stake came loose!

Free once again!

Gayelord remembered a stream near a waterfall where he could go for a dip. He didn't like all those silly people making fun of the way he looked.

So, in he slipped, horns first.

For an hour or more he enjoyed himself swimming about under the waterfall.

Now he was spotlessly clean, whiter than he'd ever been.

All that night Mac Duff worried. Where had his goat gone? Would he ever return? What would he tell all the people who were sure to come?

Next morning Gayelord appeared in all his pristine whiteness atop his little hut.

Now he was spotlessly clean, whiter than he'd ever been.

All that night Mac Duff worried. Where had his goat gone? Would he ever return? What would he tell all the people who were sure to come?

Next morning Gayelord appeared in all his pristine whiteness atop his little hut. Crowds were already waiting outside the gate but when they saw Gayelord they began to grumble. "We've come all this way to see a plain ole goat!" someone complained. "Who said we'd see a miracle? It's a hoax, that's what it is!"

Instead of being dismayed or angry, Mac Duff was glad to have his goat back, even without his coat of many colors. Miz Phipps helped take down the banner.

Mac Duff hopped in his truck and drove off to the village for supplies.

and when he came back he had a surprise for Miz Phipps,-- a brand-new set of beautiful water colors!

He also brought back a present for Gayelord.
Now Can you guess what it was?

Yes, a nanny goat to keep Gayelord company!

They had fun butting into each other all day long which of course sometimes is a sign of great friendship and affection between two goats.

And so together they lived scrappily ever after.

Crowds were already waiting outside the gate but when they saw Gayelord they began to grumble. "We've come all this way to see a plain ole goat!" someone complained. "Who said we'd see a miracle? It's a hoax, that's what it is!"

Instead of being dismayed or angry, Mac Duff was glad to have his goat back, even without his coat of many colors. Miz Phipps helped take down the banner.

Mac Duff hopped in his truck and drove off to the village for supplies.

And when he came back he had a surprise for Miz Phipps—a brand-new set of beautiful water colors!

He also brought back a present for Gayelord. Now, can you guess what it was?

Yes, a nanny goat to keep Gayelord company!

They had fun butting into each other all day long which of course is sometimes a sign of great friendship and affection between two goats.

And so together they lived scrappily ever after.

*Don and Lydia
in his studio*

About Don Freeman

In 1951, Don Freeman published his first picture book, *Chuggy and the Blue Caboose*. In a career that would last until his death twenty-seven years later, he wrote and illustrated thirty-one more picture books, creating some of childhood's most enduring characters. But Don's drawing career began twenty years before he started his first children's book, and it nearly didn't begin at all.

Although it's hard to believe now, Don was not always set on a career as an artist. Born in San Diego in 1908, he loved jazz and the trumpet his father had given him for his tenth birthday, which he taught himself to play. He also loved theater, and would stage plays in his backyard. However, was also an inveterate sketcher who used to draw the customers in his father's clothing shop.

In his autobiography, *Come One, Come All,* Don wrote of the moment his official study of art began. Standing in line at his high school graduation, he was handed a telegram. Don recalled, "I imagined its contents: STEP OUT OF LINE CALCULATIONS SHOW DISCREPANCY IN GRADE MARKING MAKING IT IMPOSSIBLE FOR YOU TO GRADUATE." But instead, the telegram contained his

grandmother's invitation to spend the summer at the San Diego School of Fine Arts, which, for Don, was an "irresistible enticement."

After getting a basic grounding in drawing, illustration, and anatomy, Don felt he could no longer put off making a living. So he hitchhiked across the country, playing one-night stands on the trumpet to support himself. He wrote, "Once in a while I found myself torn between a life playing the horn and a life using the pencil. Whenever I heard Bix Beiderbecke play cornet solos on the latest recordings I would have put my soul in hock to have been able to play hot licks like his."

In the fall of 1929, Don landed in New York City, where he supported himself playing the trumpet while he studied at the Art Students League and took painting class with John Sloan, whom he credited as one of his great influences. "Mr. Sloan encouraged us to feel as free as possible in interpreting the figure as long as we were not influenced by the 'photographic.' 'The camera can't think!' he said. 'It only photographs lies.'"

Don's second great teacher at the League, Harry Wickey, taught lithography and etching. Don wrote, "I found that the lithographic medium fitted my temperament to a T-square. The sensitive surface of flat stone was so rewarding that it set me to work translating into prints all the random sketches I had gathered about town. Now my weekly calendar read something like this: Lithographing in the morning, painting in the afternoon and Broadwaying at night." Besides his formal training, Don went everywhere with a sketchbook. He said, "I had to keep drawing to let the world know what wonderful people I had come across."

Don loved New York. He wrote, "Instead of feeling like a stranger I began to feel as if we had known each other all our lives. Everyone was accepted on equal terms. . . . Everything demanded to be recorded, and my great worry was that the dimestore supply of sketchbooks might run out."

Years later, after he moved with his wife, Lydia, to Santa Barbara, his enthusiasm for New York was undiminished. He said in a 1968 interview, "We live in a sort of a mountain cabin. When someone asks me about it I just say, 'It's beautiful—but I don't mind it!' I'm a city guy. . . . I only need one bush or one tree—out there I have too many. People keep me going. My hobby is living."

As for Don's trumpet playing career, it had ended abruptly in the early 1930s. "One night I was coming home on the subway and was so busy sketching I didn't realize it was my stop until it was almost too late. I lurched out of the train, the doors closed behind me, and I realized I had left my trumpet inside. I know it sounds melodramatic, but there I was pounding on the door. Losing my horn made me face the fact that I would have to make my living by drawing. I started submitting work to Arthur Folwell, the editor of the *Herald Tribune* Sunday section. My work kept piling up on his desk as Mr. Folwell found it quite resistible. Then one Saturday night when I

was walking up Eighth Avenue, I bought a Sunday paper, and there was one of my drawings printed on the front page of the drama section!

"Had the drama editor known what a weekly pest I was to become after that, he would probably have reconsidered using this first drawing. Every Monday afternoon at four, for the next several years, I appeared at his desk loaded with material gathered from my adventures through the stage doors of all the current productions. Having ecstatically crashed into the theater with this one drawing, it was almost unbelievable to me that such a privilege could also be a way of earning a living—seeing the plays and being paid for it at the same time!"

Don had met his future wife, Lydia Cooley, in art school in San Diego, and in 1931 she came to the city to visit him. He wrote, "The city in all its grimy glory helped me win over my girl Lydia to my way of life. It was love at first sight between her and the city and soon afterward we

were married. . . . Our honeymoon was spent revisiting all the places I had written Lydia about. She had to see Mulberry Street, Orchard Street, and the Bowery, and of course Broadway."

For the next twenty years, Don worked primarily as an illustrator for the drama departments of the *Herald Tribune*, the *New York World*,

and the *New York Times*, and for *Theatre* magazine. He also illustrated William Saroyan's *My Name Is Aram* and *The Human Comedy*, and did the color art for James Thurber's *The White Deer*.

About the regular work he did for the *Herald* Don noted, "The drawings were paid for by the column; in other words, if a drawing stretched across three columns I would be paid thirty dollars, ten a column, which may account somewhat for the tendency of my compositions to take on a rather wide rectangular shape!"

After the birth of their only son, Roy, Don and Lydia created a book for him called *Chuggy and the Blue Caboose*, and a librarian, Marjorie Rankin, encouraged them to get it published. In an interview in 1968 Don said, "Since [*Chuggy*'s publication], I've been hooked. I can create my own theater in picture books. I love the flow of turning the pages, the suspense of what's next. Ideas just come at me and after me. It's all so natural. I work all the time, long into the night, and it's such a pleasure. I don't know when time ends."

Don wrote and illustrated thirty-two picture books in all—and many of them were completed in hotel rooms. He often checked into a hotel as a deadline approached, in order to avoid distraction. "I've finished books in hotels in San Francisco, Los Angeles, New York City, and a host of other big cities. *Dandelion* was done in a gloomy hotel room in Washington, D.C."

When asked if he had any advice for budding writers and illustrators of children's books, Freeman said: "Never try to imitate any other artist or illustrator. *Never write down to children.* Never assume that children are less intelligent or insightful than they are, simply because they are children."

Don died in 1978 at the age of sixty-nine. *A Pocket for Corduroy* was on press at the time of his death, and he also left behind several unfinished works. One complete work, *Gregory's Shadow*, was discovered among his papers and published in 2001.

In 1979, reflecting on their long collaboration together, Viking editor Linda Zuckerman wrote: "Don's approach to a picture book never really changed with the design trends of the time. His pictures were always free, spontaneous, and

sometimes a little sketchy. We tried occasionally to put them into a frame, to suggest borders. But Don's unpretentious, down-to-earth, old-fashioned approach never varied. His books are not glamorous, but they are honest. And they will remind us by their worn bindings and their smudged pages that the child is the final judge and that the children of the world have given Don Freeman the highest award—their loyalty and love."

Sources:

Anne Commire. *Something About the Author,* Volume 17. Gale Research Inc., 1976, pp. 60-69.

Don Freeman. *Come One, Come All.* Rinehart and Company, Inc. 1949.

Chronology of the Life of Don Freeman

1908   Born August 11 in San Diego, California, the second of two children.

1915   Following his mother's death, he and his brother, Warren, are placed with a guardian, Mrs. Blass. Their father visits once a week.

Late 1920s   Studies art at the San Diego School of Fine Arts following high school graduation.

1929   Hitchhikes from California to New York City, playing the trumpet to earn money along the way.

1929-1930   Supports himself in New York by playing the trumpet while studying art at the Art Students League.

Early 1930s   Loses his trumpet on the subway one night and realizes he has to earn a living by drawing. Begins submitting sketches for publication to the *Herald Tribune* Sunday section.

1931   June 30, marries Lydia Cooley, an artist he met in San Diego.

1930s   Drawings appear regularly in the *Herald Tribune*, the *New York Times*, the *Christian Science Monitor*, and *Theatre* magazine.

1940   William Saroyan asks him to illustrate his book *My Name Is Aram*. Three years later he illustrates Saroyan's *The Human Comedy*.

1945   Illustrates James Thurber's novel *The White Deer*. Publishes *It Shouldn't Happen*, a book of cartoons based on his experiences in the Army during World War II.

1949   Only child, Roy Warren, is born in Santa Barbara, California, where the Freemans had returned to live.

1951   Writes and illustrates his first children's book, *Chuggy and the Blue Caboose*, with Lydia. The book is published the same year.

1953   Wins the *New York Herald Tribune* Children's Spring Book Festival Award for *Pet of the Met*, his second book, written with Lydia.

1958   Receives a Caldecott Honor for *Fly High Fly Low*, published in 1957.

1964   *Dandelion* is published.

1968   *Corduroy* is published.

1973   Publishes his twenty-fifth picture book, *Flash the Dash*.

1978   Dies February 1, at the age of sixty-nine. *A Pocket for Corduroy* is in press at the time.

Source:
Anne Commire. *Something About the Author.*